To my Grandmothers, I love you.

"Soulmates come in the form of friends too, it's not just about romance. Sometimes, it's your best friend who makes you feel whole and who understands you the most when the world doesn't understand you at all."

Sylvester McNutt III

When I was younger, my grandmother would always tell me stories about Mångata. She was not Swedish, but she had a book full of words lost in translation. Mångata is a Swedish word which translates to "moon-road". It is the road-like reflection of the moon on the water. I always felt like the word was so poetic. Grandmother used to say "When you are lost, look for the Mångata and there my child you will be found".

I have never felt this lost before. It may sound dramatic because I am only 13, but I am lost. Nothing is the same. Every day has become this vicious cycle that I feel trapped in and the one person I used to tell everything to, I can't.

What if I go to the Mångata to be found, but when there I am not found, but truly lost forever?

They say you can't choose your family, but on August 5th 2007 I did. I chose Eleanor, and she chose me.

We were born within an hour of each other, but because I was born at 11:34 pm and she was born at 12:03 am, I'm older by 29 minutes. Which also means we just missed out on having the same birthday, which we both agreed was for the best. Eleanor is my best friend, but we have two very different personalities.

Our dads have been best friends since they were children, so we were going to meet either way, but I like to think that it was fate that brought us together. Eleanor is my chosen family, and I'm hers.

We live in Milton Keynes, the city of roundabouts. Well technically we're still a town, but I'm not about to get into that whole debate. That doesn't matter to us; we just call it MK. MK is not booming with things to do for young people, but we get by. For a small town/city, we sure do like our lakes; and Eleanor, and I have a particular lake that we like to call ours. I'm sure it's many peoples' lakes, but we like to believe it's ours alone.

Our parents have stopped asking where we're going because they know that we're always at the lake; they only ask that we be home before sunset. Every day my parents remind me that I have to be extra cautious because I'm a girl, let alone being a black girl. I always carry around a personal alarm, and my mum has taught me some self-defence moves, just in case. Like if someone covers your mouth, yank their pinky back or knee them in the groin. I don't plan on getting attacked, but nobody does, so it's always best to be safe.

"Jayla, Jayla did you hear me?"
I was in my head again; I didn't even hear her.
"Oh sorry, I was completely out of it, what did you say?"
"I said, should we start heading home?"
"Yeah, we should. The sun's going to set soon, and we don't need our parents having a go at us, again."
We both chuckle, remembering what happened last time we were a few minutes late.

I continued laughing, long after she stopped, lost in the memories.

"Where do you go?"

I heard Elenor make a noise and snapped out of wherever I went.

"What? Sorry I...I didn't hear you emmm, what did you say?"

"I said, where do you go?"

"I don't know. I guess I got lost in the all-consuming consciousness that is me"

Eleanor looked at me straight-faced and shook her head.

"You've been reading too much John Green again haven't you?"

"Yeah, I definitely have."

We both laugh again.

"Come on you weirdo."

We both picked up our bikes to ride home, and when Eleanor bent down, I saw her touch her head like she was in pain.

"Are you ok?"

"Yeah mate, I'm good, just a headache, you know how I get them. There's no need to worry."

Before I could respond, Eleanor was on her bike shouting back to me "Last one home's a rotten egg". I shook my head, picked up my bike and tried to catch up to her.

Today was just like any other day, but for some reason, I felt a veil of unease fall over me while we were cycling home, but I'm sure it was nothing, just my mind playing tricks on me.

Once we got home, I still felt uneasy. I don't exactly know what the feeling was, maybe dread. Eleanor waved goodbye to me, but I couldn't even muster up the strength to wave back at her. I wish I had.

"Mate, what's going on?"
"I don't know what it is, but I just feel like something bad is about to happen."
"Like what?"
"Like something life-changing."
"Like I'm about to get a boyfriend and stop hanging out with you."
"No, not like… wait what?"
"Lol mate you know I'm just messing."
"Hahaha very funny."
"Well there's no need to be sarcastic, it could happen."
"No, it couldn't."
"Yeah you're right, I'd never leave you for a man."
"For a boy."
"For a man."
"For a boy, we're only 13; these boys aren't men yet."
"Facts!"
We both laugh.
"Seriously though, Jayla what's going through your head."
"I…"

The moment I opened my mouth to respond to Eleanor thoughtfully, her mum came into her room to tell her it was past her bedtime and took her phone away.

Whenever my heart feels uneasy and I can't fall asleep, I pray.

In Jesus' mighty name, Amen.
Lord, please help guide me because I am currently lost, and I don't know why.
I feel like something terrible is about to happen, and I'm unable to stop it.
The last time I felt this way was right before grandma passed, and I don't think I can go through something like that again.
I can't sleep, and I couldn't eat. My soul feels restless, and I'm anxious about Eleanor.
I was afraid to tell her that the feeling of dread I felt was toward her. I don't know what this could mean, but I pray for her health and overall well-being.
In you Lord, we live, move and have our being.
Oh, and I pray for peace because you're the only one who can grant me true peace of mind.
In Jesus' mighty name, Amen.

I wish I could go back. Back to the days where life was fun, and we'd go to the lake and be kids. Where death was a concept we couldn't quite grasp, let alone experience. Where death only really happened to older people who had experienced what life had to offer. My life changed, within a number of hours, and I was helpless to it. I couldn't save her, no one could. A death like this comes like a thief in the night, giving no warning and taking no prisoners. Eleanor was a casualty to the universe, to fate, and I'm mad as hell.

I haven't cried. It's been six months since my best friend died, and I haven't cried. I haven't been to church because it's clear, God doesn't answer my prayers. I haven't been to our lake, and I refuse to find myself at the Mångata as Grandma told me to, because I don't want to be found, I'm content with being lost.

My parents started to worry, so now I've started to see Dr Daniels, a Grief counsellor. I didn't want to go, but it wasn't like I had a choice. I've been prescribed antidepressants and some other pills that I'm not taking. My parents think I am, but I don't want to. I like feeling this way; it's the only way it feels like Eleanor is still here. I haven't been able to speak to Eleanor's parents since the day they came to my front door, to tell my parents that Eleanor had passed away in the middle of the night from a brain aneurysm.

She complained about another headache and had started to wear her glasses more because her eyes were hurting, so her mum suggested she go down to get a glass of water. Her parents heard glass shatter. By the time they came down to the kitchen, there was nothing that they could've done. She had suffered a brain aneurysm and on her way down had hit her head on the kitchen counter. Even if, by some miracle she had survived the aneurysm she would've died from the fall. Her parents found her on the kitchen floor, dead. I'll save you the gory details, but now every time I see the colour red, I feel like throwing up.

Her parents tried to talk to me at the funeral but I just couldn't. I couldn't write her eulogy either. I know that it's selfish, but every time I see her parents, I see her, and if I talk about her and finally open the flood gates, I'm afraid they'll never be able to close again. So now I'm reduced to a state of numbness, which I've accepted.

In loving memory
of
Eleanor Lei
Beloved Daughter, GrandDaughter
and Best Friend
You Will Be Missed

06.08.2007 - 13.02.2021

Dr Daniels says that I must "go through the ritual of saying goodbye", in order to let go fully, but I don't want to let go. Dr Daniels and my parents have told me that I'm in denial. That's probably the case, but I don't care to fix it. By admitting that she's dead, I'm accepting the fact that my best friend, my soul sister, is gone, gone forever, and I refuse to do that.

I came to the lake for something. I don't know what. I didn't tell my parents I was leaving; I just left in the middle of the night with my bike. I didn't consciously know where I was going but found myself at the lake, in our spot. This sadness felt like an ocean that I was drowning in. I just needed something, some sort of sign that I wouldn't always feel this way. I looked out at the lake and saw the Mångata. Walking along the Mångata, I saw an angelic figure. Without thinking, I ran into the water to see what it was. I ran too quickly and slipped.

I slowly opened my eyes and looked around and saw I was
on the Mångata, and Eleanor was standing in front of me. I
looked down and saw that my winter clothes had changed
into a shimmery floor-length dress.

"What is this?"
"What do you think this is?"
The being that looked like Eleanor
spoke and I jumped back.
"How is this even possible?"
"Well, you're in the space between."
"Between what?"
"Worlds, reality, consciousness…"
"And how did I get here?"
"I think you know how."
Wait I'm in the lake, I must be drowning.
 So is this a hallucination?
"Yes, you're hallucinating."
"How did you hear that? I thought that"
"We are in your consciousness Jayla;
I can hear every thought and feel every
feeling."
"Ok, so what am I feeling right now."
"Anger"
"Well, you lied to me!"
"I know."

"You told me that it was nothing!"

"I thought it was nothing."

"That's a lie, and you know it!"

"I didn't want to worry anyone. I felt something was off, but I didn't think it was that serious."

"You died!"

"I know."

"You said we were in this thing together, but you lied, you said you were ok, but you lied, you are a..."

"Can I speak now?"

I gestured for her to speak.

"I wish I could tell you that I felt a warm light shining on me as all the Angels came to meet me at the golden gates of the afterlife. I wish I could say I was whisked away by a beautiful angelic being who rode a nearly blinding white unicorn. I wish it were that dramatic, but much like my life, my death was pretty ordinary. One minute I was amongst the living, the next I was with the dead. I didn't leave you on purpose, and I think you know that"

"I'm just so angry. How could something like this happen, to you of all people? Not only were you a good person but also a good daughter, a good best friend, a good Christian.

Why did God take you away from me?"

Tears started to stream down my face for the first time since Eleanor's death. Eleanor smiled gently and wiped the tears from my eyes.
"Impossible, I am unforgettable.
You will always remember me;
I just do not want you to
get lost in remembering"
"Now look who's been reading too much John Green."
We both laughed.

"Oh Jayla, it was my time."
"How the hell could it have been your time, you were 13 years old!"
"I have completed my purpose on this earth. I know it's hard for you to understand and at first I was confused because I haven't lived my dream, but then I found enlightenment. I now know the mysteries of the universe, and it is vast and beautiful. My life served its purpose."
"I...I don't know what to say"
"It's time to say goodbye, dear", a familiar voice that was not Eleanor's spoke.
"Wait, who was that?"
Eleanor smiled, and a hand at the start of the Mångata reached out towards Eleanor.
"That was your grandma; she knew you would come to the Mångata in time."
"In time? In time for what?"
"It's time for me to pass over fully. I held on as long as I could because I knew you needed me."
"I don't want to let you go; I don't know-how. I don't want to forget."

"I actually prefer the classics like Austen and Brontë; they are some cool women."

"You've met... don't tell me."

Eleanor smiled softly again as the hand started to get closer.

You are so much stronger than you know, and you have not completed your purpose yet. Go back to church, pray because you know in your heart that when you pray, you are not only closer to God, but closer to me. You are the strongest person I have ever met, and you will not just get through this, but thrive! It's time for you to go back now."

"No, I am not ready to say goodbye."

"You just did. Now it is time for me to sail away on the lagoon of souls into the infinite sunset.

Can you imagine, they have a lagoon of souls and an infinite sunset, but they gave me the most basic death."

We both chuckled.

"This isn't goodbye."

"Of course, it's not. This is just a temporary separation. Whenever you're lost come to the Mångata, and you will be found and when there is no Mångata, look up at the sky, and you will see your grandma and me. We'll be the brightest stars shining."

"I love you."

"I love you so much, but now it's time to breathe."

"What?"

"You need to breathe!"

I woke up with a start in my mum's arms.

"What... what happened. Why are you wet?"

My mum sobs.

"Are you ok?"

"Yes, mum, I'm fine. I'm actually much better."

"You ran away, but I knew the only place you could be. Why were you in the water? Were you trying to get yourself killed?"

"I admit I've been in a pretty dark place, but I saw Eleanor and heard Grandma. Everything is going to be ok now."

"You jumped into the lake! You saw who?"

"Yes, I did and I saw Grandma and Eleanor. I'm sorry. I wasn't thinking. But now I am, and that will never happen again."

Mum cupped my face.

"You're going back to Dr Daniels."

"Okay"

"And you're going to start taking your prescribed medication."

"Okay"

"And you're going to start talking to me because you can't keep bottling everything up."

I grabbed my mum's hand.

"I will, I promise."

"Come on, let's get you dry."

We both stood, and I looked out at the lake. The Mångata is gone, but in its place are two bright stars. I squeezed my mums hand and said, "Eleanor and Grandma are going to be okay". My mum squeezes my hand back and says "And so are you, Jayla". At that moment, I knew I would be because I have not completed my purpose. I am here for a reason, and I intend to live every day like it could be my last because it very much could be.

It's been a year since it all went down. I started coming to the lake again because I realised by not going I was only punishing myself. I was angry for a long time after Eleanor's death; I guess a part of me still is. But after that vision/hallucination, which the doctors say was caused by me inhaling too much lake water when I slipped, I feel a sense of peace every time I think of Eleanor. Almost like she's right next to me, I could touch her if I just reached out. Wishful thinking I guess.

The morning after the whole almost drowning incident, there was a knock on my bedroom door, and it was Eleanor's parents. At first, I didn't know what to say, and neither did they, so we all just stared at each other blankly. They eventually sat down on my bed, and for the first time since Eleanor's death, things almost felt normal between us. They had come over to give me a playlist Eleanor had made for me the night she passed away. She had planned to give it to me the next day, before. The playlist was called "Jayla's ultimate playlist for feeling sad, happy, depressed and hopeful". There was a note attached to the playlist. I'll never share what exactly she wrote because those words are between us, but they will forever act as a beacon of hope. A part of me thinks she knew what was about to happen, and this playlist was goodbye—a way of leaving a piece of herself with me.

As a tribute to Eleanor and the awesome playlist she made me, I wrote her a sing. I titled it 'The Way We Were'.

I now go down to the lake to listen to the playlist and to sing the song. The opening lyrics always stick with me, "I miss our daily coffee, I miss our inside jokes".

Things won't ever be the same, but hopefully, one day I won't get so lost in remembering and like Dr Daniels says, "finally master the art of letting go".

One day, I will.

Acknowledgments

I would like to thank my family for their support and encouragement throughout this process. You helped keep me level headed and for that, I am grateful.

A big thank you to my amazing illustrator Olivia Yap Li Wey. You brought my vision to life and I am so appreciative of all your hard work.

Thank you to my best friends past and present, you have helped shape me into who I am. The good, the bad and the ugly.

Lastly, thank you to you the reader for taking the time to read my book. This book was a labour of love and I hope you enjoyed it.

Helplines

Serious and upsetting themes are discussed in this book. Below is a list of organisations that you can get in contact with to seek help or donate to.

Harry's Rainbow
Tel: 01908 061676
Web: www.harrysrainbow.co.uk
Email: info@harrysrainbow.co.uk

Child Bereavement UK
National Helpline
Tel: 0800 02 888 40
Web: www.childbereavementuk.org
Email: support@childbereavementuk.org

Winstons Wish
National Helpline
Tel: 08088 020 021
Web: www.winstonswish.org
Email: ask@winstonswish.org

CALM
National Helpline
Tel: 0800 58 58 58
Web: www.thecalmzone.net

Mind
National Helpline
Text: 86463
Tel: 0300 123 3393
Web: www.mind.org.uk
Email: info@mind.org.uk

No Panic
Youth Helpline (13-20 year olds)
Tel: 0330 606 1174
National Helpline
Tel: 0300 772 9844
Web: www.nopanic.org.uk

Samaritans
Tel: 116 123
Web: www.samaritans.org.uk
Email: jo@samaritans.org

PAPYRUS UK
National Helpline
Tel: 0800 068 4141
Text:07860039967
Web: www.papyrus-uk.org
Email: pat@papyrus-uk.org

Apps-
BetterHelp
Headspace
Daily Calm
Calm
Mindfulness
Reflectly
Wysa
Daylio Journal

Meet Jayla

"What if everyday we chose to do
the impossible and live?"

Jayla

Definition of Jayla-
A feminine variant of the name Jay, which may derive from Hebrew and mean 'God will protect', or from the Sanskrit meaning 'victory' or from the Greek meaning 'to heal'.

Description-
Dark skinned Nigerian black girl with a short afro.

Style-
Girly, mature, neutral and solid colours

Height-
5"4

Age-
13 years old

Eye colour-
Light brown

Favourite song-
The Acid - 'Basic Instinc'

Favourite colour-
Navy Blue

Meet Eleanor

"Playlists are like a look into ones soul. What is your soul made of?

Eleanor

Definition of Eleanor-
Of Hebrew origin and a variant spelling of the name Eleanor which comes from the Hebrew element 'el' meaning 'god' and 'or' meaning light, so the name means 'God is my light' or 'God is my candle'.

Description-
White/Chinese girl with a wavy bob and full fringe, wears glasses and has vitiligo, a condition in which the skin loses its pigment cells.

Style-
Quirky, Childlike, prints and bright colours

Height-
5"2

Age-
13 years old

Eye colour-
Deep green

Favourite song-
Moira & Claire - 'Mind Over Matter'

Favourite colour-
Burnt Orange

Jayla's ultimate playlist for feeling Sad, Happy, Depressed and Hopeful

Drum & Lace - 'Dame That's Good'
Yebba - 'Where Do You Go'
The Acid - 'Basic Instinct'
Gold Brother - 'Part of Me'
Konradsen - 'Odd Mistake'
Nicholas Britell - 'Agape'
Camille Saint-Saëns - 'Carnival of the Animals: The Swan'
Claude Debussy - '2 Arabesque, L. 66: No. 1 in E Major'
Kyoto Harp Ensemble - 'The Path of Wind'
Balmorhea - 'Masollan'
Arlo Parks - 'Hurt'
UMI - 'Lullaby'
Cleo Sol - 'Still Cold'
Sabrina Carpenter - 'Exhale'
Ama Lou - 'This Town'
Moira & Claire - 'Mind Over Matter'
Dizzy - 'Twist'
Chelsea Williams - 'Fool's Gold'
Billie Eilish, ROSALíA - Lo Vas A Olvidar
FINNEAS - 'Angel'
Clare Bowditch - 'When I Was Five'
Frida Sundemo - 'The Sun'
Jessie Reyez - 'LOVE IN THE DARK'
Frida Sundemo - 'It's OK'
Ruelle - 'The Other Side'
Billie Eilish - 'i love you'
Anna Hauss - 'I Can't Remember Love'
Bea Miller - 'i can't breathe'
Grace Carter - 'Why Her Not Me'

FINNEAS - 'I Lost a Friend'
Arilssa - 'Healing (Acoustic)'
Ben Platt - 'River'
Tori Kelly - 'Before The Dawn'
Harry Styles - 'Fine Line'
Kate Bush - 'This Woman's Work'
Dizzy - 'Twist (Piano Version)'
Angrlo De Augustine - 'Tomb'
Ruelle - 'Game of Survival'
Shanks Mansell - 'Love Is Contagious'
Georgia - 'Started Out'
Aly & AJ - 'Potential Breakup Song'
Hayley Williams - 'Simmer'
Killing Roy - 'Applier'
Cathedrals - 'In the Dark'
Tei Shi - 'Bassically'
MØ - 'Kamikaze'
Grouplove - 'Tongue Tied'
Emilie Nicolas - 'God Damn'
Asaf Avidan - 'Different Pulses'
Flume, kai - 'Never Be Like You'
CLAY - 'Sponge'
Ariana Grande - 'ghostin'
Ruelle - 'War of Hearts (Acoustic Version)'
James Arthur - 'Train Wreck'
Bon Iver, St. Vincent - 'Rosyln'
Nao - 'Orbit'
Emilie Nicolas - 'Roots'
Gracie Abrams - 'Stay'
Selena Gomez - 'De Una Vez'
Sufjan Stevens - 'Fourth of July (Live)'

My special song for Eleanor

The Way We Were

V1
I miss our daily coffee
I miss our inside jokes
I miss the friend I use to know
I miss the way we were

Pre-chorus
I keep feeling like time is gonna change things
But time can't change your fate
It keeps me up at night, remembering,
Such a cruel, cruel fate

Chorus
I miss you
I miss the way we were
I miss the feeling
I miss having my go to
I miss you
I miss you everyday

V2
Summers come and gone,
Winters here
Chilling me to the bone
I wish you were here

Pre-chorus
I keep feeling like time is gonna change
things
But time can't change your fate
It keeps me up at night, remembering,
Such a cruel, cruel fate

Chorus
I miss you
I miss the way we were
I miss the feeling
I miss having my go to
I miss you
I miss you everyday

Bridge
I've started loosing memories
Pictures are getting blurry
I feel you all around me,
But I can't quite grasp, the feeling
I'm loosing all my senses
Life was better with you in it
How am I suppose to heal
When you took my heart, with you

Chorus
I miss you
I miss the way we were
I miss the feeling
I miss having my go to
I miss you
I miss you everyday

Outro
Yeah I miss you
I hope you miss me to

Song credits
Written by Jadesola Omole
Performed by Jadesola
Produced by Jadesola Omole

About the Author

"Time's funny because you can't control it, only decide how you spend it…"

Jadesola Omole

Jadesola Omole was born and raised in London. Growing up in a home filled with loving parents and siblings allowed Jadesola's creativity to flourish. An active imagination can be a powerful tool and she took full advantage of hers. Jadesola's passion has inspired and motivated her throughout her life and is what led to her writing, blogging, painting and photography.

Music has been a constant staple in Jadesola's house, while growing up. From her Dad playing Luther Vandross on repeat in the car to her oldest sister blasting songs by Paramore, The Killers, Kings of Leon, and many more all around the house. This inspired Jadesola to start making music and earn her Bachelor's degree in Music Business.

Jadesola thrives each time she hears a perfect note or lets her fingers drift over the keyboard. Though singing and songwriting remain her top priority, her love for writing has grown and flourished into this book.

The main thing Jadesola wishes for readers to take away from her work is how friendships come in different shapes and forms. Jayla and Eleanor are best friends, but Jayla also has a strong connection with her mother. Mångata beautifully shows how human connections help people grieve, heal and grow.

Contact Details:
Instagram- @jadesola_music
Website- www.Jadesola.co.uk